The
GRAND CANYON
Doesn't Scare Me

Written by Dennis Fertig
Illustrated by Andrea Kantrowitz

STECK-VAUGHN
A Harcourt Company

www.steck-vaughn.com

CONTENTS

CHAPTER ONE

My Adventure Begins

When I started this assignment, I thought it would be easy. I was supposed to write a report on Arizona's landforms, and I'd seen plenty of them last summer. That's why Mr. Hoffman gave me the assignment. But when I started to write, other stuff kept creeping in—like how nervous I was about flying for the first time, funny things my grandfather said, and the scary adventure I had in the Grand Canyon. Mostly I kept remembering all the reasons why I'm tougher than Lizzie Lopat. The more I thought about all these things, the more I wanted to tell the whole story about my Arizona trip. I asked Mr. Hoffman if my landform report could be a story instead. He said, "Sure, Beth, as long as it covers landforms." That's how my report became a story.

Since it's a story about landforms, the first thing I should do is explain what a landform is. A landform is any part of the *land* that's *formed* by nature. Get it?

Land. Formed. Water, wind, heat, and cold act over long periods of time to make landforms.

Arizona may hold the record for the most landforms in a state. It has mountains, hills, and other things that lots of states have. It also has buttes, mesas, arroyos, and other landforms you've probably never heard about. In Arizona, you can walk, run, and climb over all of these, unless you're too scared to try, like Lizzie Lopat.

My grandparents live in Jerome, Arizona. Their house is more than a thousand miles away from mine here in Chicago. I don't get to see Grandpa and Grandma a lot. They come here sometimes. I like being with them. They're easy to talk to, hate to sit around, and really like me. They also tell good stories about when my dad was a boy.

My parents made plans for me to visit Grandpa and Grandma by myself last summer. I was happy when Mom told me. She said my grandparents would take me to interesting places all over Arizona. We would do lots of hiking and exploring because those are the things my grandparents love to do. I love to do them, too. Then I asked Mom how I was going to get to Arizona. When she said, "On an airplane," I was less happy. I had never been on an airplane before, and I was a little afraid. After Lizzie Lopat started talking to me about my trip, I was a lot more afraid.

Lizzie is weird. She is always sure that things will go wrong. Because she's so sure, she thinks it's foolish to even try things like flying in an airplane.

"An airplane by yourself?" she asked. "Flying is scary. The plane is too high up in the sky! You'll get sick when it bounces up and down in the air. Even if that doesn't happen, you'll get lost in the airport or take the wrong plane and wind up in Russia!"

That's Lizzie Lopat. She worries so much that her worries have wrinkles. I've heard these kinds of scaredy-cat ideas come out of her mouth all my life. I know the best thing to do is ignore her if I can.

Still, on the day Mom and Dad took me to the airport, I was worried about flying. In fact, by the time I said goodbye to them and walked onto the plane, I was terrified.

My seat was next to a window. No one was sitting next to me. After I sat down, the pilot announced to the passengers that the plane would be sitting at the gate for awhile before we took off. While we were waiting, a flight attendant walked down the aisle, checking on seat belts. Maybe because I looked nervous, she sat down for a moment in the seat next to me. "Hi," she said. "I'm Carla Johnson. What's your name?"

My mouth was dry, and my hands were sweating. "I'm Beth Nevarez," I croaked. "This is the first time I've ever flown."

"That's great. You must be excited," said Carla. She had a friendly smile.

"I am," I said to her slowly. Then I added, "But I'm scared, too."

Carla asked why, so I told her about Lizzie Lopat and all the scary things Lizzie had told me. I hadn't told anyone about Lizzie's crazy worries before. I'm not sure why I did then. But Carla did something that was perfect. She talked about each of the things Lizzie had said and why I shouldn't worry about them. Carla said flying on a big jet was safer than any other form of transportation. She said that if flying were really unsafe, no one would do it. She told me that hundreds of thousands of people fly every day. Millions and millions of people fly every year! "Many people, like me," Carla added, "fly several times a week and love it."

Carla told me she had flown on thousands of flights and had only seen two or three passengers get airsick. She said I wouldn't get lost in the airport either. She promised she would make sure I was in the right spot when we landed in Phoenix. Finally, Carla said that Lizzie Lopat had a terrific imagination if she thought I would wind up in Russia instead of Phoenix.

It's true that Lizzie has a terrific imagination. All the other things that Carla told me made sense, too. In just a few minutes, she really helped me to relax. I told her I felt better. Then Carla had to get ready for the flight.

A few minutes later, the pilot announced that the plane would take off soon. Carla walked past me again and stopped. She promised that during the flight, she would come by now and then to tell me more about flying—why the plane moved up or down and why it made the noises it did.

When the plane roared down the runway and lifted into the air, I felt pretty good. I wasn't too nervous. In fact, I felt happy. I was flying!

Then I realized something. Lizzie would never be brave enough to fly in an airplane. I knew that was one reason why I'm tougher than Lizzie Lopat.

CHAPTER TWO

An Unusual City Park

My first flight on an airplane turned out to be smooth and comfortable. I enjoyed the changing view outside my window. Carla stopped by occasionally to tell me about what the plane was doing. Once in awhile, the pilot used the plane's loudspeaker to tell us passengers where we were and what we could see out the windows.

When we flew over the Rocky Mountains, the pilot explained that they are the largest mountain range in North America. I knew even more. The Rockies were made millions of years ago from giant movements of Earth's crust. A long time ago, some of the Rockies were volcanoes. All the mountains were shaped by thousands of years of wind, rain, and ice.

When we were close to Phoenix, the pilot pointed out the Grand Canyon. From high in the sky, I couldn't see the Colorado River flowing through it, but I knew it was there. The river is *why* there is a Grand Canyon.

After we landed in Phoenix, Carla took me to meet my grandparents at the gate. When I saw them, I thanked Carla for helping me. Then I ran to Grandpa and Grandma and gave them each a big hug.

"Welcome to the Valley of the Sun," said Grandma. That's another name for the Phoenix area.

"Welcome to the Valley of the Granddaughter, at least for the next few days," said Grandpa.

I laughed. Grandpa is full of jokes. When he had a heart attack a few years ago, he even joked with the doctors who saved him.

Our plan was to stay in Phoenix for a few days before we drove to my grandparents' house in Jerome.

We checked into a nice hotel by a golf course, and I went out with Grandpa to watch him play golf. He said he liked everything about golf—walking, the sun, the green course—except hitting the little white ball.

That day we drove around and saw some of Phoenix. We got back to the hotel early because we planned to hike in South Mountain Park the next morning. Before I fell asleep that night, I thought about the hike. I knew Lizzie would be afraid to go. I could imagine her saying that Grandpa would have another heart attack, or one of us would fall on the rocky trail, or we would die of thirst in the hot Arizona sun.

I was up before it was light to eat breakfast with my grandparents. If you hike in Arizona in the summer, you have to start early in the morning. It's too hot to hike in the afternoon. When we got to South Mountain Park, I was shocked. The park is in Phoenix, but it doesn't look like any city park I'd ever seen. It's bigger than some towns and full of small mountains and rocky trails. Just driving through it made me wonder whether I should be like Lizzie. Some of the trails looked like sprained ankles and broken legs just waiting to happen.

When we started hiking, it wasn't as scary as I had thought it would be. I'll admit that when we first began to climb over the large jagged rocks, I was worried about Grandpa. I was out of breath right away, and I thought hiking had to be harder for him. But he is in very good shape. He wasn't even breathing hard. Instead, he made jokes about how the park looked like a rock farm.

Grandma explained what really happened. Over thousands of years the land froze and then got hot, froze again and got hot again, over and over. The constant changes in temperature broke the earth into big rocks.

As we hiked, we drank lots of water and rested often. We climbed to the top of Dobbins Mountain, where we had a fantastic view of Phoenix. We could

see skyscrapers, the baseball park, and even other mountains that seemed to pop out of the middle of the city. Those mountains were millions of years old, too. Grandma said they once seemed higher, but the land around them, called basins, filled with rocks that tumbled off the mountains. The basins flattened out over time, and people eventually built Phoenix on them. I knew Lizzie couldn't live in Phoenix. She would be sure that more rocks would fall and cover the city!

As I stood on Dobbins Mountain and thought about Lizzie, I also realized that she could never have made the climb. She would have been too afraid. I said to myself, "This is the second reason why I'm tougher than Lizzie Lopat."

CHAPTER THREE

Rushing Waters

The next day, we took a jeep tour into the desert near Phoenix. Our guide, who was also the driver, was a desert expert. As he drove us far from the city, I decided I was going to be tougher than Lizzie Lopat. I knew she would worry about rattlesnakes, sharp cactus needles, and getting lost. I was not going to think about being scared of anything.

This time, however, something scary really did happen. We were looking up at a mesa, which is a funny-looking little mountain. The mesa stood out in the middle of the desert, all alone. It had a flat top like a table. In fact, *mesa* means "table" in Spanish. Our guide said that mesas used to be part of bigger landforms, but wind and water wore down their sides over the years.

Grandpa said that what happened to those big landforms was the opposite of what had happened to

the hair on his head. "The hair on the sides is okay," he joked, "but all the hair on top has been worn away."

We were laughing when the guide suddenly held his finger to his lips and said, "Listen." Then we heard it. It was a rattling noise, and it came from a curled-up rattlesnake looking at us from about five feet away. Our guide said, "Climb slowly back into the jeep. Don't go any closer to the snake."

Going closer to the snake wasn't what I had in mind. After we were safely in the jeep, our guide explained that rattlers don't normally bite or even threaten humans. He said that our laughter must have startled it.

"Sorry," said Grandpa.

"Well, I don't mean we should be quiet," said the guide with a smile. "But no matter where people are in the desert, they should keep an eye out for rattlers, scorpions, and other poisonous creatures."

He must have seen my eyes get bigger because he added, "As long as you watch where you put your feet and hands, you're safe from those critters. They're more afraid of you than you are of them."

I thought to myself, "Well, I might believe that, but Lizzie never would. She wouldn't even get in the jeep to go on a tour of the desert. But I did. And that," I decided, "is the third reason why I'm tougher than Lizzie Lopat."

We enjoyed the rest of the tour. We saw huge cacti, rock drawings made by American Indians long ago, and an old gold mine. We also climbed on a butte, which is like a mesa but smaller and not so flat on the top. Grandpa didn't make any jokes about it.

You might be getting tired of all this landform talk, unless you're Mr. Hoffman. But if you've been to Arizona or seen pictures of it, you know how interesting some of its landforms are. For instance,

on the way back into town, the
guide drove alongside something
called an arroyo. It looked like a long, dry,
bumpy road dug into the ground. Kind of dull, right?
But the guide said if you were in the middle of an arroyo
after a rainstorm, the arroyo would be very exciting. It
would suddenly fill with dangerous rushing water!

I mention rushing water not just because of arroyos,
but also because of what happened later. Grandpa and
Grandma took me to their favorite Phoenix restaurant
for dinner. It had really good food and was well known
for hot, hot barbecue sauces. Grandma loves hot sauce.
Grandpa doesn't.

"Try this special extra-hot barbecue sauce, Beth,"
Grandma said to me.

"Don't do it, Beth," said Grandpa. "It will make your
mouth hotter than a desert arroyo at high noon."

I laughed. I thought to myself that Grandpa almost
sounded like Lizzie. I knew I had to try the sauce.

Grandma cut a small piece of her barbecue sandwich and gave it to me. I took a taste, and it was good. It was also the hottest thing I'd ever eaten. My mouth was on fire!

That's where the rushing water part comes in. I had to drink a whole glass of cold water fast to cool off my mouth. "Grandma, how can you handle this stuff?" I gasped.

"I guess I've just developed a taste for it," she said.

I don't know that I will, but at least I tried it. That's the fourth reason why I'm tougher than Lizzie Lopat. I guess it's also the first reason why I'm tougher than Grandpa—and probably the only reason.

That was our final night in Phoenix. The next day we left for Jerome, the town where my grandparents live. As we drove out of Phoenix, I tried not to think about the crazy fears about Jerome that Lizzie had come up with back in Chicago. But I was worried.

Jerome sits high on a mountainside. It's almost a mile higher than Phoenix is. The highway that goes to Jerome climbs and climbs. The highway also makes many sharp turns on the edges of cliffs. If a driver makes a mistake, it could be a big one. Back in Chicago,

Lizzie had said she was sure that Grandpa would make that mistake.

Jerome is a special town for a couple of reasons, and one isn't good. Part of it once slid down the mountain! Lizzie found out about that before I left Chicago. When she did, she was sure that even if I made it to Jerome safely, I would come back down the mountain in one horrible, sliding crash. Lizzie said she'd rather be in a car that crashed down a mountainside than in a town that did!

CHAPTER FOUR

Dangerous Curves

My grandparents own a jewelry store in Jerome, but it's not like any jewelry store anywhere else. Nearly all of the back wall is a huge window. The view from it is like the view from an airplane. You can see smaller mountains and the valley below. People in Jerome claim you can see 50 miles. Sometimes my grandparents say they should cover the window so that customers will look at the jewelry and not the view.

Grandpa and Grandma live above the store. The building is three stories high. Their house is the top two stories. It has the same spectacular view from big back windows.

I guess you can tell that my fears of Grandpa driving off a cliff were foolish. First of all, he didn't drive up the mountain roads. Grandma did. Second, people who make the drive all the time are good at it. Grandpa and Grandma make the drive all the time.

I guess it would be easy for a car to plunge over one of the cliffs on the highway. But Grandma said that the safety record for the highway is better than for most flat, straight highways. Grandpa told me why. The road is so full of curves that people must drive slowly and carefully. That made sense to me, and I relaxed. I knew that if we'd left it up to Lizzie, she would have refused to go any farther once she saw those dangerous curves. Unlike her, I was able to enjoy the wonderful views as we climbed up the mountain road. That's the fifth reason why I'm tougher than Lizzie Lopat.

Grandma explained a little about Jerome's history. The mountain Jerome is built on was once filled with copper mines. Miners often used dynamite to get to the copper. The dynamite shook up the mountain, and soon parts of the town started to slide down the mountain. The jail slid down more than two hundred feet!

The mining stopped decades ago, and so did the sliding. After the miners left, Jerome almost became a ghost town. But then artists, musicians, and writers who moved there slowly rebuilt it. Soon tourists came, too. My grandparents sell them jewelry that local artists make. Some of the jewelry is made from copper.

"When we bought this building," said Grandma, "we made sure it was safe. We had engineers check it."

"Yes, we thought a slide-proof building would be nice. If we'd wanted a house in the valley, we would have bought one there," said Grandpa with a wink. It took me a few seconds to get his joke. Grandpa meant that he didn't want their house to slide down the mountain.

Later we walked around town, and I saw the old jail that had slid down the mountain. It is still part of Jerome and always will be. That night I slept with the curtains open in the guest room and watched the bright stars twinkle in the dark night sky. My grandparents live in a beautiful town that I would always come to visit in spite of its history. That's the sixth reason why I'm tougher than Lizzie Lopat.

One afternoon Grandma and I went by ourselves to a nearby town called Clarkdale. There we took a four-hour ride on a scenic railroad. We rode an old train that snakes along a mountainside. The train took us along the edges of cliffs that hang over a river, through a long tunnel under part of a mountain, and over old wooden bridges that cross high above water and valleys of rocks and trees.

Sometimes I looked out of the window and saw how far up we were. Only the wheels on the tracks kept us from falling. Once or twice, I was so afraid that I had to close my eyes—but not for long. The beauty of the reddish-brown cliffs, the green forest, and the rushing blue river was too good to miss. The views made the scary part worth it.

Of course, Lizzie Lopat wouldn't even be able to look at photos from this kind of trip. She would never be brave enough to sit on the train. That's the seventh reason why I'm tougher than she is.

After our few days in Jerome, Grandpa, Grandma, and I drove north to the Grand Canyon. That's where I learned that sometimes there are very good reasons to be afraid.

CHAPTER FIVE

Grand Canyon, Grand Hike

The Grand Canyon is awesome! You can marvel at pictures or videos of it, but nothing compares with seeing it in person. It's the biggest, deepest thing I've ever seen. Its many layers of rock have brilliant colors— reds, browns, yellows, and even pinks and purples. Rock towers in the middle of the canyon blaze with the same kind of spectacular colors. Out of the rocks grow green trees and bushes, some with bright flowers. Everything glimmers and shines. As the sun travels overhead through the day, the look of the canyon changes, always to something more beautiful than before.

When you see the Grand Canyon in person, you also notice something else. It's frightening. It's so deep that if you fell into it while you were reading the first chapter of this story, you would still be falling! That's deep!

The afternoon that we arrived at the Grand Canyon, we walked around the top a little. We looked at the beginning of Bright Angel Trail. That was the trail we were going to hike early the next day. Our plan was to take it all the way down the Grand Canyon, camp there overnight, and hike back up the next day.

I saw two things that worried me. First, the trail looked more dangerous than anything I had hiked on. It was so steep that I immediately thought of Jerome sliding down the mountain. The trail also looked very narrow. In the distance below, hikers hugged the cliff

walls on one side of the trail so they wouldn't fall off the steep cliff on the other side.

The second frightening thing I saw was people riding mules on the trail. The mules were broad, and the riders' legs often stuck way out on the sides. I knew I would never, ever ride a mule, so that part didn't scare me. But I also knew that on our hike, my grandparents and I would have to pass mules on the narrow, high trails. I couldn't believe there would be room for both hikers and mules. I didn't need Lizzie Lopat's help to be nervous about the trails.

That night, I did what I had done on other nights in Arizona: I worried instead of sleeping. My mind was full of the same kind of horrible thoughts that Lizzie would have about hiking into the Grand Canyon— falling mules, wild animals, heart attacks, dying of thirst, and more.

The next morning, I was up early with Grandpa and Grandma. It was still dark as we finished breakfast and put on backpacks. Each backpack was filled with food, extra socks, a jacket, a sleeping bag, and other supplies, including a first aid kit. We had lots of water, too. My pack was a little heavy, but I knew I could manage it.

We waited at the top of the trail for the sun to rise. I shook with cold and nervousness until the sun started to climb over the canyon. The sunrise was so gorgeous that I forgot my fears. Before I could start worrying again, we were hiking down Bright Angel Trail.

The hiking was easy at first. Grandpa made jokes, and Grandma talked about the rocks we saw. The trail seemed wider than it had looked when we stood above it and looked down at it. I didn't walk near the edge, and all three of us walked carefully on the downward slope.

When we'd hiked for about an hour, we stopped to
rest under a tree. Experienced hikers know that rest,
shade, and water are important. While we were resting,
I looked up at the top of the trail and saw that a group
of mule riders were getting ready to start down. I knew
it wouldn't be long before they caught up with us and
passed us.

Grandpa knew I was worried. "Relax. Mules are trail
experts," he told me. But I wasn't, and that scared me.

After we'd walked for about another hour, the mules
caught up with us. We stood next to the canyon wall as
a dozen mules and riders passed. We said hello to the
riders, and most said hello to us. One rider didn't greet
us, though. He was a boy my age. All he did was stare at
the long drop-off on the other side of the trail. He was
scared. I couldn't blame him.

The mules stepped right on the edge of the trail. I
couldn't tell whether they did that because they were
sure-footed or because they weren't paying attention.

I did know that Lizzie Lopat would ride on a mule
on a Grand Canyon trail before I would. I would never
do it. Never.

Once the mules passed, I breathed a sigh of relief and enjoyed the hike. As we walked farther, I noticed that the colors of the rock layers were different from those we'd passed earlier. When we took a long break around noon to eat and to avoid hiking in the hottest part of the day, Grandma explained that each layer of rock was from a different time in Earth's history. The Colorado River, now at the bottom of the canyon, had slowly cut through the layers, over millions and millions of years. Time and the river had made the Grand Canyon so spectacular. When we actually saw the river later that day, I was surprised. I thought it would be full of boiling rapids, but it looked calm. Grandpa said it was wilder at other places.

When I say I was relaxed on the trail, I mean I was relaxed about hiking. Worries about camping at the bottom of the canyon played in the back of my mind. When we arrived at a campsite, I started thinking about spiders crawling on me while I slept. Then I moved on to worrying about wild animals getting our food or us. Next I wondered whether parts of the canyon had ever fallen on anyone. Lizzie had worried about the spiders and the wild animals back in Chicago.

Once we set up our camp and cooked dinner, I felt pretty safe. Other people camped around us, including the group of mule riders. I felt stupid about being afraid, so I decided it *was* stupid to be afraid. Soon I felt myself drifting off to sleep. "The Grand Canyon doesn't scare me," I told myself. "That's the eighth reason why I'm tougher than Lizzie Lopat."

The next morning, we ate early and started to hike back up Bright Angel Trail. It was hard at first, but after two hours of climbing, I felt good. We would reach the top before the day ended, and everything would be okay. All of Lizzie's fears—and mine—would be jokes to laugh at.

Suddenly everything changed. I heard a noise behind me. It sounded like something scratching through pebbles. When I turned to see what it was, I saw the worst thing I've ever seen in my life. Right before my eyes, Grandpa slipped and fell feet-first over the side of the cliff!

CHAPTER SIX

Tough Decisions

Grandma and I moved as quickly and carefully as possible to the edge of the cliff. We looked over and got a big, wonderful surprise. Grandpa was sitting on a rock only a few feet below us. When he saw us, he said, "Be careful. I just noticed that it's slippery up there."

"Are you okay?" asked Grandma.

"I think so," said Grandpa. But when he tried to stand up, he winced with pain. "On second thought, I think I've hurt my ankle."

Grandma and I found a safe way down to where Grandpa sat. Grandma gave him a quick hug and said, "Let's have a look."

After she'd studied his ankle and tried to move it a little, Grandma said she thought the ankle was sprained. Grandpa had scratches on his knees and hands, but otherwise he was all right. Still, it was clear that he wasn't going to hike anymore that day.

We helped Grandpa move to a shady spot near the trail. Grandma did a little first aid on Grandpa's scratches and ankle. As Grandma worked, she and Grandpa talked and decided that she should climb up alone for help. I would stay to take care of Grandpa. They said that a youngster shouldn't hike alone on this dangerous trail. Grandpa and I would be under that tree for hours, maybe even overnight.

As we talked, we heard a clopping sound from down the trail. It came closer and closer. On the part of the trail we could see below us, we soon spotted the source of the sound. The mule riders were climbing back up. They would be where we were in about thirty minutes.

As soon as I saw the mules, I knew help was on the way. But my stomach knotted with fear. I suspected I might have to do the one thing I said I would never do.

Eventually the mule riders made their way up to us and stopped when they saw we were in trouble. It was the same group that had passed us yesterday.

The guides in charge, a man and a woman, looked at Grandpa's ankle. They were trained in first aid and both thought it was a bad sprain but not a break. They also decided that the best thing for Grandpa, Grandma, and me was to ride up to the top of the trail with them. Worse than that, they said we would ride two to a mule. They said this as if it were no big deal.

I was terrified and asked why Grandma and I couldn't just hike up. The guides said it was already late in the morning, and we had a long way to go to the top. Besides, they were sure that the shock we had felt when we saw Grandpa slide off the cliff would make the hike harder. One of the guides said, "That experience will make you more tired than you expect."

Grandma patted me on the back and whispered, "Don't worry. The mules can handle all of this." I don't know how people can always tell when I'm afraid.

The guides decided that each one of them would take an extra rider. Grandpa would ride with the male guide and Grandma with the female.

35

While they were deciding where I would ride, I noticed the boy who was so terrified yesterday. He looked calmer now. "They wouldn't make me ride with him, would they?" I wondered. They did. Before I could argue, the guide was lifting me up on Old Surefoot, right behind the boy. The guide said, "Your partner is Brendan. He's turning out to be a real mule expert. You'll both do fine."

"Mule experts aren't named Brendan, and kids don't become experts overnight," I said to myself in a panic.

Brendan said to me, "I was a little scared yesterday, but Old Surefoot is a good mule. If he weren't, they wouldn't put two kids on him. Don't worry."

The mules in front of us started climbing up the trail. Brendan held the reins of Old Surefoot and gently nudged the mule to start. I held onto Brendan's waist tightly. My legs were clamped just as tightly onto Old Surefoot's sides. I saw Grandpa with the guide on the mule in front of the group. Grandma was somewhere behind me, but I was too scared to look back.

After we had climbed farther, I worked up enough courage to look around a bit. I shouldn't have. We were nearing a narrow ridge that wrapped around a high cliff.

Anybody or any mule that fell off the ridge would never climb back up again.

I grew more frightened as we got closer to the ridge. When we were finally there, I tried not to look over the edge, but I couldn't help it. It was terrifying. All I could see was my foot sticking out on Old Surefoot's side and then a long, long drop. I wanted to climb off Old Surefoot and curl up in a little ball on the trail.

Yet Brendan seemed unconcerned and even enjoyed the view. Old Surefoot took strong, even steps.

After we traveled that narrow trail, I took a deep breath. Old Surefoot had taken us safely along the edge. I knew he could take us all the way up. I won't say that I enjoyed the ride, but I trusted Old Surefoot.

When we climbed over another narrow cliff-hugging part of the trail, I thought about Lizzie for the first time that day. Of course, she wouldn't ride a mule. She'd be paralyzed with fear. But here I was riding Old Surefoot up a narrow Grand Canyon trail. That's the ninth reason why I'm tougher than Lizzie Lopat.

In a few hours, we were at the top of the trail. My grandparents and I thanked the mule riders for their help. Then we went to the hospital. The doctor said Grandpa did have a broken ankle! Of course, Grandpa joked about it. "I guess I won't make the Olympic soccer team this year, Beth," he said.

In spite of Grandpa's injury, I enjoyed the rest of my Arizona visit. When it ended and I was on the plane back to Chicago, I got a little nervous. But compared to riding Old Surefoot up the Grand Canyon, flying didn't seem scary at all.

Guess who was a flight attendant? Carla Johnson! I told her all about my trip. She said, "I'll bet you can't wait to tell your friend Lizzie about Arizona."

I had forgotten that I told Carla about Lizzie. I also realized I hadn't thought about Lizzie since I climbed off Old Surefoot. Then I decided to tell Carla something that no one else knew. "Carla, there is no Lizzie Lopat."

"There isn't?" Carla looked surprised.

"No, she was me. My name is Elizabeth Lopat Nevarez. *Lizzie* and *Beth* are both nicknames for *Elizabeth*. Lizzie was the part of me that was always afraid. Beth is, well, me."

Carla smiled and said. "It sounds like Lizzie isn't flying back to Chicago with you."

It was true. Somehow I had said goodbye to Lizzie on Bright Angel Trail. I no longer needed her to tell me what could go wrong or that I should be afraid. I would always have fears. Everyone does. But I wouldn't let my fears make my decisions.

And that's the tenth reason why I'm tougher than Lizzie Lopat!

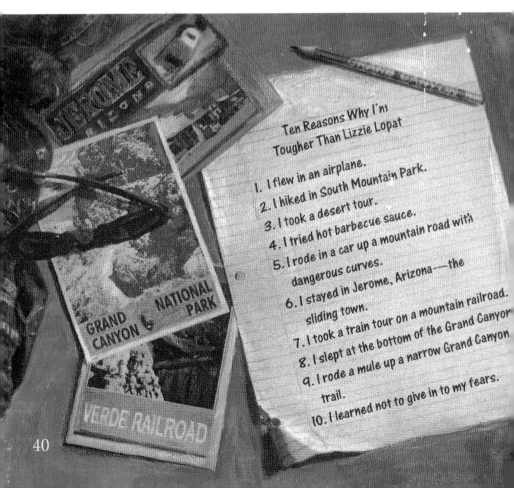

Ten Reasons Why I'm Tougher Than Lizzie Lopat

1. I flew in an airplane.
2. I hiked in South Mountain Park.
3. I took a desert tour.
4. I tried hot barbecue sauce.
5. I rode in a car up a mountain road with dangerous curves.
6. I stayed in Jerome, Arizona—the sliding town.
7. I took a train tour on a mountain railroad.
8. I slept at the bottom of the Grand Canyon
9. I rode a mule up a narrow Grand Canyon trail.
10. I learned not to give in to my fears.